THE LONG, SLOW SUMMER SUN

P. VOLK

HAIIRO PRESS

CONTENTS

INTRODUCTION

I have a penchant for the dramatic.

I think that this developed over time through a childhood consisting of few friends, many books, action figures and video gaming. There weren't very many kids on my street, and those very few children who lived there typically spent the days at odds with each other for some silly reason or another. I was typically in the middle and had to choose between playing with one friend or the other. I was also overweight and a little short in the self-confidence department, and, well- you know how kids can be. And so was born the less-than-social, solitary fat kid with an overactive imagination.

Perhaps it served me well, after all.

I have not travelled this country much in my life, but have wandered over it (and others) endlessly in my mind, and devoured countless pages about a myriad of topics of fact and fiction. I've spent as much time watching and thinking, bouncing from topic to topic, as many have spent travelling the globe, and without regret.

This book has taken many turns as I sat with it over time, and I'm hesitant to delete anything that I've written because I want to not only present the "me" as accurately as I can but give you some sense of the changes in said "me" over time. I've reviewed everything here many times in the hopes that I have accurately captured the time in which I wrote a particular piece, and have rarely edited anything that I've written because I feel that it destroys the original mood and thought process. Quite frankly, sometimes I think that I have wrecked more than I have improved with each review. I'll of course edit the preface to each entry as necessary, but the core of the original blogs, poems, thoughts, memos- what have you- remain largely intact, for better or for worse.

I have also changed the names of people and locations to keep with the anonymous nature of this writing. I can't say why, exactly, I chose to collect these writings anonymously; I think that perhaps it simply fits my (melo)dramatic personality. It excites me to think that there will be a book out there that people may enjoy and share, and no one would know the true source of the work. I fancy that perhaps some day someone will approach me and say, "I just read this book by this guy Volk," magically returning the dollar that I wrote on years ago, back to me. I accept that there may be a day when I finally say, "OK, ok- I did it!" but today is not that day.

It is my sincerest hope that as you sit with this book, you take something with you as you read, and that it stirs you in some way. I assembled this diary or sorts not so much because I'm concerned with fame or recognition, but in the hope that it affects people and elicits reflection and change in their lives, in whatever way that may be. One thing against which I have always fought, as I wandered my tiny portion of the planet, is a life of endless bouncing from job to job and place to place, being consumed by the quest for endless piles of Chinese plastic junk or a full bank account (which would never happen because it can never be full enough to satisfy greed), to die empty and spent. If I can add any bit of laughter, sadness- any emotional response to break the reader from the mundane or expected- I have done my job and am satisfied.

As a side bit of trivia: for most of this book's development, "Fur and Phoenix" was its title. There was a picture that I had in mind for the cover- one I took myself, and which fit the title perfectly- until the book began to form and I noticed that I used the phrase "long, slow summer" on more than one occasion. I love that phrase, and it seems to fit for a book of ramblings much better than my first choice. "Fur and Phoenix" is only fitting for those who know me and my penchant for abstract weirdness and random statements, and even then- I found it a strange way to present this, my first book, to the world. Perhaps as you read on you'll see where the original title would have been appropriate for the text.

You'll also notice that there are short prefaces to many of the offerings in this book. At one time I thought that it would be a good idea to give some essays a little bit of context by adding those prefaces, in the hopes that you may find them more meaningful if you knew the background of the story. At this point in the book I don't know if it was a wise thing to do, but I should probably leave well-enough alone, so to speak, before I hack these perfectly good pages into oblivion

And with that- read on and enjoy.

ONE

POEMS AND LORE

I'm loosely calling the following collection "poems," though I'm not the most gifted writer of such, as I'll mention periodically.

―――ele―――

Squeak

I've written mostly overly dramatic diary-style nonfiction with a small smattering of "fairy tale" when I'm feeling emotional, which is fairly regularly. I usually grab hold of a thought or a mood and sit with it for a few minutes until my mind starts to move it in whatever direction it chooses, at which point the conversation with myself starts, and what I lovingly call "vomiting on the page" begins.

I mention this because contrary to that free-flowing random style of writing, I was forced to take a second-level English Composition course to complete my degree, which was much more structured than what I was used to, and required organized writing. Needless to say I balked at it, trying pretty consistently (annoyingly) to get out of it with any number of excuses: "I'm X years old, for crying out loud! Who needs to know how to cite works using MLA?!?" or "I've been writing for over X years. I even have a blogging site! Isn't that writing enough?!?"

Yes, I am a child.

I anticipated that it was going to be the worst class ever, but ended up being relatively enjoyable, and I scored a 102 out of 100 in it <cough> <brag> <cough> because of a 10-point extra credit assignment that I felt that I needed to do to make up for my lack of formal research skills. Ironically I really didn't need much skill, and the course was, overall, a positive experience.

One of our weekly tasks was to journal into a diary of sorts, choosing one topic from a short list, to give us some focus and start us off. I think that what I liked about this was that I could "turn on the creative juices" but with a set plan in place- a destination in mind- which I found helpful because sometimes I write and just travel this weird, winding path until I'm tired of writing, and afterword I don't often like to review what I've written because it's usually a one-time rabbit hole, if that makes any sense. It's very difficult to revisit what I've written with any thoughts of improving upon it because that fit of mental effort has passed, and usually cannot reproduce that frame of mind accurately.

Anyhow, I wanted to produce something that was essentially the passage of time marked by a sight or sound, and since sound seemed to be easier to describe and produce on paper, I chose that. I remember reading a lot of Stephen King in my day, and in particular one piece where he used something similar to trigger a sequence in the book; I don't remember the book, exactly, but the tool that he used impressed me. I'm not claiming any skill even close to Mr. King's work here; I just mentioned it because I remembered it, and for no other reason.

This work morphed into two phases, for two separate projects, and I'm not sure which version I prefer. The story originated as an odd poem (listed first), which I wanted to depict as just fast random thoughts that were tied together by a sound. The poem version is not a favorite because I don't like the way I explained the noises in each verse; I think that I could have done a little better with it by implying the noises more, but I need to leave it alone before I make a mess of it. As usual, I'm scouring over what I wrote yet again, and am not as impressed as I was the first time I wrote it, and need to put the digital eraser away, lest I make more of a mess of this thing!

As I review the second piece again, I have to admit that I found myself moved to silent tears as I read it. I dearly hope that it will elicit from you even a fraction of the emotion that it still does, from me.

Enjoy.

———ell———

< squeak >

the metal swing arcs higher in the long, slow summer sun, warm breeze of endless days

< squeak >

Harley groans, the roaring wind through my helmet and a plume of dirt down the country road

< squeak >

squad freezes, tense in the dry desert night as the old shack's floorboards betray us

< squeak >

my bride giggles as I lay her down on the marriage bed, and our eternity begins

< squeak >

worn and wise, the desk chair voices its concerns in a lamp-lit smoky den, as tuition comes due

< squeak >

whiling away the day, watching the grandkids from the window, baseball game on the radio, La-Z-Boy springs counting time

< squeak >

hospice turns down the railing, sad eyes downcast in respect, all of my life remembered to me in a sound

＿ell＿

< squeak >

I love this swing-- a big-ole worn tire under the gigantic elm tree in the yard next to the house. I could swing on this all day, back and forth, up and back, over and over again, sometimes leaning back so far that I was sure that I would smack my head on the dirt beneath it, magically summoning my mother from the screen door in a rush of ponytail and apron.

I can almost hear her calling now from the porch, "Ben! It's time for supper!" but it's not time to be done so I pretend to not hear. I'm flying, I'm Superman, Up, Up, and Away, to reach the clouds and

< squeak >

defy the laws of gravity and make other kids' parents gasp when the swing went so high and the chains went limp for that endless second as the playground swing reached the top of its impossible arc, and everyone thought for sure that I would tumble off that swing. "That Ben is CRAZY," I'd hear some of the school kids say. "He's going to bash his brains in- I know it!"

But I never do- nope, not me. I'm a big boy, and no stupid swing is going to hurt me! Mom always said that I was going to be a pilot, and no pilot was ever hurt by a swing- that would just be silly. Pilots fly high, and spin around and do loop-de-loops, shoot down the Evil Commies, and land their super-fast jets on ships in the ocean. Who ever heard of a pilot falling off a swing? They

< squeak >

check the mirror to make sure that there aren't any cops behind me as I put the pedal to the medal. I love this old Chevy- she still has plenty of kick, a V6 under the hood that says this old pick-up truck will GO when I want it to. She's fast, she's beautiful, and she's all mine. There isn't a straightaway between Hartsville and County Q that she hasn't screamed down, tearing up road and dirt, her old, weary seat springs moaning slightly as I'm pressed into them as the truck speeds down the road. MY road.

How fast am I going? Well, I don't know because the speedometer doesn't quite work all that well; it says that I'm going 55 miles an hour, but I know better. And I bet Sheriff Hughes would know that, too, if

< squeak >

he called out, apparently irritated that I didn't answer the first time because I was, again, off in the clouds. "Mr. McIntyre, will you PLEASE illuminate the class with the answer to the problem? Clearly your smile tells me that you already know it, of course." Professor Higgins flips the chalkboard around again, purposely hiding the work that he had just recently completed, smug little grin on that fat, hateful old face of his.

This guy is tricky; you need to pay attention in his class, because he favors those blasted old portable chalkboards. <FLIP-CREAK> now you see it! <FLIP-CREAK> now you don't! Rolling out the answer to his problem as flippantly as I do just now does nothing more than infuriate him and delight the class. Sorry, sweetheart, you didn't get me this time; it'll take a little more than that to

< squeak >...< squeak >...

surprise me. I can hear her footsteps coming down the hall, but I need to pretend that I do not; she has prepared this covert operation for days, and it would destroy her if she knew that I already knew about it. I must play this little game, for you see- I have a surprise in store for her, myself: I'm going to propose to her tonight.

We both completed active duty in the same year, and now that life has settled down slightly, we can begin to prepare our time a little more predictably. I favor the outdoors, and she is more of an indoor type, but we knew from the beginning, during our tour in Germany, that we were meant to be together, whatever that meant, in whatever time and place. And as it turns out, that time and place has arrived sooner than we would have thought, and is a welcome sight. I have already begun to price out homes in the area since I have steady work, and we'll have our time together to

< squeak>...< squeak >...< squeak >

sit on the porch and enjoy our quiet neighborhood. I love this neighborhood, and I am blessed to share it with the woman I love. We sat countless times on this porch, talking and laughing, and sometimes just sitting and staring at each other, and I marvel at the beauty of the woman who has chosen to spend her time with me, and wonder why this goddess has chosen me. She is bold and witty, strong yet completely feminine. She is an Irish queen. "What have I done to deserve this woman?" I wonder, as I rock with her in the long, slow summer sun-sun as bright as her fiery hair. I thirst for

< squeak >

something to soothe this parched throat as I almost knocked over the IV cart next to me, this rickety thing making all sorts of noises. Damned tubes and wires! This Cart from Hell will surely be the

< squeak >

"...death of me!" so I'm told by the nurse as she raises the back of my loud, old rented electric bed. We have had many such conversations about life and death, and that is fine; I know that I have lived a full life, beyond my peers and everyone that I have loved, and I enjoy engaging the nurse in some intelligent conversation. Sometimes, though, in the middle of my sentences, she is gone. I don't know where she went- why she suddenly disappeared only to return (is that even the same uniform?)- but she does. Odd behavior for someone who is supposed to be with me all day.

Time has passed so fast, and I have so few memories that my mind's eye can see, yet sometimes I sense them. There's a picture in my sparsely-decorated room-- a painting of a modest house in the country, with a grand tree and a tire swing in the yard. I like looking at that painting; to me the light changes, growing more golden to almost glow, but I know that this is my old eyes playing tricks on me. I sense warmth and love in that picture and get lost in it somehow. Strange.

My nurse stops talking and touches my shoulder to comfort me from time to time, because sometimes I weep when we talk, and do not know why. She is such a nice traditional freckled Irish girl- a bold and brash young child, but respectful all the same, as of course she should be. She's a good caregiver, kind yet sharp of wit and tongue. We'll talk, and suddenly I'm overcome with some deep and aching anguish, and she raises that blasted noisy bed to prop me up for a drink and to calm me down, which always works. Sometimes my heart aches when we talk, even about the most inane things. Something is missing, sometimes it's like there's a hole in my chest, in my heart, but I don't know why.

Then she lowers the bed, and I am lulled to a peaceful rest, smiling again as if I know something, but I'm sure that I don't....

< squeak >

Who Do I See

This poem seems strangely out of place here to me now, but I want to include it, anyways. Every time I read it I can almost grasp the feeling of it, but it's elusive, and I'm no longer the same person who wrote that. I can't remember when I wrote it, or why, but I'm going to deposit it here, for whatever it is worth. This is probably, quite honestly, the least favorite of my writing. I recognize that this is partially because I wrote it before I became a Christian, and I think that the person I was when I wrote this is now dead, and I cannot identify with him or his thought process, anymore. As an aside- some day I'd like to record my conversion, because every one is special and worth discussing. But not today.

Who do I see? Not an easy question for someone with such a limited vocabulary! Smart, funny, witty, vibrant, responsible, compassionate, merciful- all a little inadequate, a little empty. It has been said that "the name that is a name is not the Name, the way that is a way is not the Way." This is entirely true. What I can tell you is *what* I see.

Faith, distrust,

Goodness, immorality,

Deity, demon,

Goodness, malevolence,

Love, hatred,

Mercy, malice,

All share one thing- irrelevance.

Love- impotent concept to which we cling,

Manmade, another box in which we cram our grand energies,

Convenient to stamp a brand on them, constrain their true being, insulting,

For the purpose of making them easy to relate to the ignorant and worthless.

We are becoming One,

Beyond human words,

Beyond your Good and my Evil, only called so because mortals

Need to mark all that they store in those puny comfort boxes.

Fear drives the weak to what caresses, lest they become

Overwhelmed in their own small-minded stupidity.

Worthless tools to be used, broken, discarded at a whim.

Choose the words you wish, they reveal the same-complete inadequacy.

We are becoming stronger,

Our true Powers evolve, growing, complementing their opposites.

Our beings dance around the Center, now complete.

There is no Good or Evil, Dark Gifts or Divinity. Humans need those concepts.

There is Energy.

Power.

Yours.

Mine.

My anger tempered by your empathy.

Your wisdom soothing the sting of my aggressions.

Your times of indecision led to the path by my pointed swiftness.

My stone sharpens your blade as your spirit cools the metal heated by my fire.

Perfection.

Balance.

The Way.

Learning To Give

I'm sure that I mentioned before that structuring poetry is far from my forte; I enjoy writing it, but I tend to make the lines long, with too much punctuation. I think that my thoughts are too long for a crisp, concise poem, and maybe I simply shouldn't try to jam what I write into one.

That's how I feel about this poem, written for the college writing course that I mentioned before and am sure I'll mention again. I've gone over it a few times already and I fear that if I continue to review it, it'll never make it to print, so I'm going to leave it as it is now, for better or worse.

———ells———

because the thing that you scoff at

may be another's treasure

because the ten minutes

that you could have spent

with that old woman on the bus

instead of ignoring her greeting

and scrolling through

your shallow social media

could have given her hope and a smile

because the lane you blocked for miles

in passive aggression,

lane markers ticking time in the reflection

on the windshield

may have just counted down

his father's last breaths,

a frantic trip to the hospital

that ends in heartbreak and sorrow

because when that door closed

on the person behind you

it closed on her desperately lonely heart

for all time

because a Savior knows what humanity needs

and counsels such

because when your own life's door closes

it is good for someone to remember

a shoe

a bus ride

a door opened

because in all the span of time

you may change the course of history

and save a life

perhaps your own.

The Unfinished Adventure

A long time ago there was a boy in a small village who was just a little different from the others. He was smart but overweight, and forever made fun of by the "normal" boys who played sports and learned about cars and spitting. It could be said that he did learn about spitting, but not from being on the spitting end of it.

He spent a lot of time reading and playing, often alone, and devoured stories of knights and dragons, and samurai and soldiers of ages past. There was something fantastic yet familiar in these stories, and as that boy grew, he knew that he was to be one of them.

Now, the man with a heart for glory and battle had a difficult time in this world, because battles were not fought for glory, honor, and the princess, but for money and what people believed was power, but actually was not. He fit in well enough but was never accepted by the other males because he didn't see things like they did and didn't fight for the same prize. Men were twisted beasts, clawing for money and dress hems in spurts of drunken courage, smelling of weakness and bile, and he would have none of it.

So across the land and the ages this man wandered- an odd man always standing apart from the rest, often seen with a random mischievous grin for no apparent reason (and we can imagine that he was again fighting some battle or another, if even only in his imagination).

As the years went on our man had fought for various causes, and championed the Horde as his adopted "people," undoubtedly for their battle cries of honor, strength, and death before defeat, and the deep family bonds of the Frostwolf clan. Strange but somehow fitting for our misplaced warrior.

In one of what can only be a miraculous and divine twist of fate, our tireless warrior stumbled across the most beautiful and amazing princess he had ever set his eyes upon. Strong and fierce, yet so tender and vulnerable to the keen eye- a true woman to be treasured and fought for at any cost. He had never seen in an earthly being such a combination of vigor, sensuality, strength and sensitivity, and doubted that she was, indeed, of this earth.

His heart pounded at every glance, and his breath was caught up in his chest every time this angel appeared before him. He knew that he had finally found the woman for whom he would fight- and die- if necessary. She was not only worthy of such a man, but appeared to be made for this man, and he for her, because he knew that though strong and able, she desperately needed to be fought for, and won, so that she might put down her own arms and rest.

One day-

(This tale remains unfinished, for I cannot see the future. I didn't want to just write anything to make it complete; that's not my way.)

Who Will Remember?

There are days when I feel that something is missing from my life- some point to it that I know exists because I can barely feel it tugging at me, but it has been elusive. Then there are days that it doesn't matter- I have made my choices in life and have tried to stay true to my convictions, so wherever I am is where I am and I can die here. I don't believe that I'll be remembered by more than a small handful of people, and that's usually fine.

Usually.

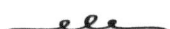

Who will sing your lifesong through the tomorrows?

Who will see your smile in a flower in the garden, and leave a fond tear on a petal?

Who will teach your favorite song to the breeze on a long slow summer evening?

Who will scream your name to the heavens?

Who will remind the day of its purpose- that it was for you, that it began?

Who will remain in years to come, eyes squeezed shut, desperately hunting for the color of your eyes in the slides of the mind, as time fades the ink of memory?

The saddest love song is that which, unsung, remains.

A Poem to My Enemy

This was also written during my semester of the legendary English Class from Hell; I chose "a poem to my enemy" from a list of topics for the week's journal. I had some fun with it, and I hope you do, too.

O Joy of My Life, I can still hear the sound of your voice;

dulcet tones, soothing to the stomach, like Taco Bell.

Your laugh sends chills down my spine, as a thousand nails

grinding a chalkboard.

I miss you today, and every day; there's a guard rail

between your face

and my car

that keeps us apart.

I count the days until we meet again and I see your smile,

counting them in the M&Ms I place in the bowl for you.

Which one is the chocolate laxative? They all look

so much alike....

I see your eyes, so bright and beautiful-

a slate blue that pales the steel of the anvil

that I have saved for you

in my mind.

You are the Road Runner to my Wile E.

I shall never meet one so unique

a light of the world

whose condescension is matched only by your

need to be right,

and the size of the insecurity

that makes you act so.

We shall never see that light again.

That's too bad.

This Game We Play

This game we play.

The look that lingers just a bit too long in passing. So brief, yet an eternity that pierces your very soul- almost too painful to bear, yet powerless to break. But why would you, for there's nothing else for you in this world.

A twinkle, a life in the eyes that wasn't there a moment ago. Life has changed just then- in an instant- and so does the dance. A laugh, a pause and a breath- a sigh? - and the most fleeting glance at the ring hand, that took just a bit too long to not be noted.

There is so much to notice, so much at stake for those who participate.

And who would not?

Why else do we even breathe, but for this game we play?

Give

Give until you are spent

then give some more.

Exhaust yourself in kind words

warm hearts

and selfless gestures.

Give intensely and with passion

and in this

know that nothing can be taken from you

that you freely give.

What A Man Wants

What does a man want? Interesting question- to find what stirs the soul of a man.

A man wants for his queen.

To shoulder her burdens

and shield her from the storm.

To be her breath, to captivate her,

and hold, safely, her captured heart.

To honor her with deeds

of strength and courage,

relentlessly,

to fight unceasing for her name

and die at her feet,

the loyal warrior and servant.

The Gift

Every person in your day is a gift.

They are a soul, a seed.

How will you treat this gift, and how

will you help it to flourish?

Every life leaves you

with your impact forever

stamped upon it

and it is your choice,

the form that impact takes.

Every Soul

Every soul is a hand,

every hand molds the heart,

and the heart guides

the man,

the wolf,

the warrior.

Two

JOURNAL

I've kept what I suppose may be called a journal or diary of sorts (though "diary" just sounds wrong because my writings rarely, if ever, gush on about a woman, and I'm not a teenager), if you call a fit of thoughtfulness recorded, a journal. I've regularly called what I do "vomiting out" whatever is in my head at the time, because, like vomiting, it's often in uncontrolled fits, and not necessarily pleasant.

I'm honestly not sure how to classify these writing "fits"; I don't believe that I can take full credit for being a good writer when it takes some effort to produce anything that may or may not be worth the paper and ink. I can pretty comfortably classify myself as an idiot savant of sorts- minus the "savant."

These entries are in no particular order, though perhaps they should have been; they may have told a better story if I placed them chronologically- but that's impossible for many reasons.   But, then again- maybe they would not have; my head moves around randomly, and the love I write about today can easily turn into the despair I scribble down tomorrow.

I suppose you'll have to judge whether these should have been recorded, or just reflected upon for a bit, then sent to the winds.

To The Mom

In my walk as a Christian, I have had many ups and downs, ebbs and surges in how "connected" I feel to God, and what He wants from me. In all honesty- I rarely, if ever, know what I am doing or why, or where it will lead me. I'm often at a loss for my next step, and I suppose I do things "my own way."

This, I've learned, yields mixed results.

I can't blame God for this, because I freely admit that I am not the best Believer in the world; I don't pray as often as I should, I'm sure, and have read the Bible in fits and spurts, which does not foster a healthy relationship with my Father. I have, however, religiously <snicker> tuned in to Thru the Bible with J. Vernon McGee, a radio show hosted by a gifted man and teacher.

There are times, though, when my orders are clear, and those times are sometimes both exciting and intimidating, because I know that I am not going to be in control of what I am doing or where I am going- and I do NOT like that. You'd think, given what I usually call my "violent" salvation, that I'd know better, and trust God to do with me what He wills, but nope.

The following short blog entry was a vivid example of one of these times; I had no idea what ultimate purpose this would serve, or when, but I knew that I needed to do this. Ooh- I just had an interesting revelation: what if the entry from the past was designed to be published here, and affect the future from this point, rather than the day I originally posted it?

Mind blown.

I don't always get to know why I need to follow a directive, or its purpose, but when I receive one- I am certain that I did. I know what my God wants of me right now, but I don't know why. Please share this as you think you need to, or not at all; it's not up to me to know what is going on. All I need to know is that I do it:

To the mom who lost her son to his country,

To the mom of the hero in blue,

To the mom of the estranged,

And those who succumbed to sickness,

To every mom who knew her boy but can't hold him any longer,

for whatever reason.

You need to know this:

"I love you mom."

<Author's note: there was a picture of a vase of roses that I bought, inserted here.>

I will keep these healthy for as long as I am able.

Take care of yourselves.

The Lesson

As I wander I learn, and many lessons are difficult, but I think that none of them are accidental, and every one of them is necessary. As is proven now and again- my Guide is wise but merciless, but I'm thankful because these lessons taught with tears and blood remain eternally.

I need these ramblings- to record my "wisdom" in blogs and squares- because there are so many of them, and in this moment they seem so important to me that I need to immortalize them, I suppose even just for myself, for who else can appreciate these tired and torn thoughts of a generally unremarkable man? I cannot say, and it doesn't matter; these inane musings go on paper, one by one, for another day's recollecting, and perhaps a laugh or a sigh. I'll put one on a blog, and another in an Instagram square, and save it for later, as if it's somehow important.

Today my Guide throttles me down the path of joy and pain, travelling together and continuously, as is usual in these adventures. I hear the pressing message clearly, or better said- I can feel it as it is burned into me. The message is two-fold:

The Dalai Lama has said, "Be kind whenever possible. It is always possible."

I have said, "There are two impressions that you will leave on a person- positive or negative. There is no in between, and it is up to you which one you leave."

There is so much to do here, so much to learn, and so much to say. These lessons come from near and far-

hopelessly far and out of reach- in heart-wrenching depth and all too frequently. Every soul is a hand, every hand molds the heart, and the heart guides the man, the wolf, the warrior.

Another lesson. Another square. Another tear.

School Is Out

This goofy collection of blog entries was designed to be, and briefly became, a video blog. I recorded them just after the end of a semester of college, which, when combined with a full-time job, hobbies, and gaming, made for a busy life, and such an abrupt pause in schoolwork caused a somewhat traumatizing lack of busyness.

The series has since been removed from the Internet. Had I more regular content I would probably have added them to the regular blog site, but I never ventured to maintain such a site. People have said that I can talk (take that however you choose), but I dont' see myself as a vlogger.

I absolutely do *not* claim this series to be any brilliant work of literature- and I also believe that the videos were much more entertaining than these entries. It can be difficult to get a proper sense of a person's personality in printed text, and these entries were never designed to only be read; they were merely written as a script. I'm including them in this book for the sake of "full disclosure," good or bad.

And I apparently have no shame.

—ell—

Dear Diary : first morning of No School Books. I started reading cereal boxes, but bulk warehouse club cereal boxes don't have fun stories written all over them like the ones you buy at a normal grocery store do. Lots of long words, though. I think I'll learn how to pronounce them all. Maybe learn their molecular structure. This should take a while.

Hour Twelve of No School: the 3D model mapping out of the ingredients in Cap'n Crunch came to a screeching halt; I ran out of crunch berries, marshmallows, and toothpicks. I got up to thiamin mononitrate, but had to stop. Now I'm hungry and have no cereal.

And ironically, I also just got something stuck in my tooth.

No Classes, Day Two: I dismantled the models of the Cap'n Crunch ingredients, in favor of making macaroni necklaces. Unfortunately I put the cart before the horse, so to speak- I hate fishing, and have no fishing line. No fishing line- no macaroni necklaces.

Day Two, Late Afternoon: I was able to locate thread, and decided to continue the macaroni crunch berry necklace project.

(Later) prototype testing update: it rained- I'm now wearing a soggy macaroni sharktooth necklace and it looks like a clown threw up all over my shirt. Project halted.

Day 3: the Cap'n and I had a discussion. I admitted that I'm not sure that I know how to relax.

"DUH," he replied.

The Cap'n- always brutally honest. He knows me.

About 7,188 Seconds into No Classes: I began noting the time in seconds and have become a tad obsessive about counting them during the day. I wonder how the seconds are pronounced in other languages, because they pass by faster than it takes me to say them.

I think I may need to develop another language.

Nu Zed Nooknits into No Derfba: I have developed another language to accommodate the counting of nooknits in this flerb. I think that it will go vorpily once I ook the splanken just a little. It's too mooma to tell at this niik.

Day 6: I decided to braid my hair. I'm not sure how it'll go, because my fingers are fat and I continuously drop the tweezers. Maybe I need longer hair; I don't think a buzz cut is conducive to great braids....

Day 7: hair braiding project shifted from head to chest hair, which is much easier and longer for braiding. I was able to finish, but I feel a little awkward with all of these little pokey things sticking out under my shirt.

Day 8: I have been thinking about developing a line of mood clothing. I'm not sure of the logistics of that, though, because I'm not an expert clothing tech, and don't know how to change the color of clothing. I don't know how practical it would be to carry all of the moods in a bag as an alternative, while on the go, either.

What If I Fly?

"'Tis better to have loved and lost than never to have loved at all." - Alfred Lord Tennyson

Oh, is it, now? That's the question of the day.

There are a lot of people at the gym today, and up on the elevated back row of treadmills I can see them all. There's a mix of ages, and more women than usual today, which probably triggered this resurfacing of some recent conversations and random musings. Or maybe it was the sound of the iron, an outward reflection of this recent inner battle.

I can't help but feel a little sad as I look around.

I don't know what she's hiding, or the source of her pain, but I know it's there in varying degrees. I don't know who has buried her heart to keep it safe, but I do know enough to know that, with some, it may never be found again. I see her poised in watch atop her wall, faithfully standing guard in the rain that masks her tears, and that breaks my heart, but I can't pretend that I am not, or won't be, the reason for such a tragic watch.

I wish that I could sum, pound for emotional pound, the risk involved in living freely versus the energy and happiness lost forever in the careful guarding of the heart and soul, but I can't; my eyes are too fresh to see clearly, and my own heart is a young and stupid child, and can't know or understand. Today it screams out to live, and live mightily, but one would be foolish to trust a child, no?

Or maybe the child has it exactly right.

Perhaps some day I'll look back upon all of this written nonsense with the answer. And tonight, right now, I don't know that I'd like that answer because I fear that it leans towards the preservation of the heart, which ironically is what is causing me such pain today.

The Awesomeness of Self

I have just returned from a getaway weekend, and I have to say that it was one of the most interesting and life-changing little vacations that I've taken yet. I can't say that I understand all the implications of it, but I'm fairly certain that it is related to me just "being me" and in an unfamiliar place.

I can be outgoing and a bit chatty under certain circumstances, but this vacation was unique in that it was the first time that I had the chance to live in whatever "new head" and new plan I've been cultivating- or more accurately: the new me that has been piecing itself together without my interference, which may be the key this time. Life changes constantly, and I'm all over that, BUT it usually changes in places I've seen, in doses that I can handle, and among people I know.

But not this time.

I was "on my game" for the entire trip and made it a point to relate to people more "deeply" than usual, which essentially means asking more personal questions, and sharing more of my own life than usual. Granted: the majority of these conversations was with waitstaff, retail, and hotel personnel, but that didn't matter- everyone had a story to offer, and everyone was about to hear one.... No one left my presence without a gift, a name, a compliment, a story- whatever- and everyone smiled (some by my leaving the area, I'm sure). And as if to put the final stamp of approval on this little adventure, I was entirely taken aback by a compliment offered to me, quite spontaneous and by surprise, as I ended my vacation. It was on my "style," and no one talks about what I wear- no one. Maybe we are the only two people who appreciate what I was wearing, but hey- validation is validation.

I think that some of this "life-changing experience" might just be only in my head. I work in an amazingly negative and unhealthy environment; mostly everyone around me is miserable, complaining, or mad, and I am often the recipient of the venting of this anger and misery, though rarely if ever the cause. I know- "Waah, man. Deal with it." I do, and it rolls off me to a point, but I think that perhaps this is why I am so surprised when someone is kind, smiling, or complimentary. It's just foreign. In an average day someone has probably told me what I should or should not be doing or saying, and most certainly has complained about someone else.

"But I digress," so they say.

At any rate: this was my weekend to set myself loose upon a strange part of the planet, in the company of complete strangers, yet in my most comfortable location or natural habitat- the mall setting. And run rampant, I did. I over-tipped, over-gifted, chatted, complimented, schmoozed- what have you. And not with any sinister or selfish intent; I just had the chance to blurt out all the "unfiltered me" that there was to be blurted. If I appreciated someone's hair- they knew about it. Great with kids? Informed. Awesome piercings? You had better believe they were told about them. It went on and on, endlessly and tirelessly. From the hotel, to restaurants, to the mall and beyond: I'd like to think I'll be remembered, if even as the weird old guy who talked to much. As an aside (as if this whole story isn't one!): did you know that, with typically only one direct and personal question, someone will tell you a story? I think they need to, and the secret only lies in knowing the correct question. A lesson in attentiveness and observation.

Not everyone can handle the full force of a Me in Motion, but if nothing else- everyone was gracious, perhaps even just to get me out of the area. Now the challenge for today onward is to keep this moving every day, in my home territory where I know the people and their attitudes, and the stores, and the shortcuts home. Somehow I think that this is not out of reach, because first of all: I'm not tired. And secondly: I remember the peoples' names, and I never remember.

If I have found the "me" that I am supposed to be, after 49 years, then I consider myself lucky because I'm comfortable being this person, and I am grateful because I'm not sure that everyone does.

In keeping this moving lies the challenge to Do the Awesome.

Challenge accepted.

The Johnstons

Many times in an average week (given what I suppose is my "openness to life" and what it wants to tell me) I'll just stop and be taken by a vivid memory, random and usually unrelated to anything that I'm doing. I think that generally these are triggered by a smell, or visual cue of some sort- something that has a similar pattern to what I have experienced before, if that makes any sense. I don't know if it's just me or if it happens to other people (I've never asked anyone), but there are patterns in life- roads, tree belts, hillsides, etc.- that are very similar in different places, and which trigger that same pattern memory from the past.

...or maybe I hit my head as a kid.

At any rate- if I'm lucky enough to have the time and space to write those memories down, I do; otherwise they're typically gone forever.

The Johnstons. Everyone in the neighborhood recognized that name, and I'm sure the same image comes to mind for all of them: old sisters, always on the porch, sitting (and swinging? I honestly can't remember) in their comfortable porch furniture, watching the world go by.

I never really knew how many of them there were, only that there was always- *always*- at least one or two white-capped heads (no, they weren't Blue Hairs. And what is that even, anyways?) visible behind the screened-in porch on my street. I grew up roughly across from them, and from barely the time after the last frost, to just before the first snow, they were out there keeping an eye on the neighborhood. I only remember one name- Rosalyn- but there were many sisters living there; I want to say that I remember three or four at most, but these memories are easily 40 years old, and they fade with time.

What has not faded yet, though, is the imagery surrounding that house and those sisters. I remember the low-cut shrubbery that ran the length of their property, marking a fence line at the sidewalk. I remember the nondescript bushes that lined the front of their modest two story house, but absolutely not blocking their view; I think they were rhododendron bushes, but I can't be sure. I know that there were a few of whatever the "standard" deciduous trees were in this part of the country, very tall and broad, and spaced just far enough apart to not crowd each other yet supply a constant canopy over my banana-seat bicycle riding adventures. I would ride my bike on both sides of the street because I was careful, and usually crossed just before the Johnston's house so that I could catch just a whisper of whatever conversation they were having, but could never quite hear anything. Maybe they weren't talking at all, but just enjoying the day.

What I remember most vividly- and this isn't necessarily tied to that family, but the area itself- is the quality of the light and air. My Man Vocabulary can never quite do it justice, but: the air was almost visible, as if just after a rain (and why is it visible then? I have no idea, but I can see it), and the world is golden and glowing. I hear no sound, and remember no breeze, but see the house and its trees and bushes surrounding it, all aglow with gold, as if an artist dabbed the scene with gold or yellow, yet the paint didn't smudge anything but made it clearer.

My Sock Life

Sometimes life lessons are taught in the most unusual places, by the most unusual things.

Like socks.

Now just to preface: I have a collection of what I call my "cool socks." I have a little Marvin the Martian, a little Deadpool, some ugly Christmas socks (I won't even tell you about my latest sweater!), and the like. I like my cool socks, and they elicit some great looks at the gym; I fancy that these looks, especially from the jug-of-colored-liquid-toting types, are looks of admiration and respect.

Anyhow: this morning I chose the Darth Vader socks, for no conscious reason whatsoever (or so I thought). I went about my normal routine, and as I was grabbing my boots, I thought: oh no! If I wear boots, no one will see the socks! Dilemma!

However, quick-witted and caffeinated, I thought- wait a minute: I can make a t-shirt of a picture of my socks. Now one need ever be deprived of the greatness of an excellent sock, just because of the season. WINNING. ...except that I didn't have enough time to make a t-shirt, and now the problem of "who wears t-shirts in the winter" becomes the issue. I DO have a penchant for wearing an untucked and unbuttoned flannel shirt, though, which lends itself nicely to wearing a t-shirt underneath the shirt.

Food for thought, this idea. I'll have to package this little goodie alongside my Wearing the Same Thing Everyday idea. More on that at another time.

Then it occurred to me in a Blinding Flash of Wow: I *am* the sock!

Sit with that for a bit.

I am the cool sock...and the boot is the Boot of Life.

Yea- see? You're darned right, "Whoah."

How will I choose to live? Will I let the Boot just smother my awesomeness, or will I prevail? What am I prepared to do, and how am I prepared to present myself to the world? This entire morning's event- tiny and seemingly so innocuous and inane- has the potential of changing the course of my life, forever.

I must find the courage- I must make a way- to be that ugly sock. I will be the best ugly sock that I can be. And you're just going to have to deal with it.

Mind blown.

What Are You Prepared To Do?

There's a Creed song, "Hide," in which the songwriter asks what a person will do with his or her gifts. It's a great song, and the questions are burned into my head like the afterimage of the sun, and the answers are "everything," as far as I can discern.

I have been blessed with a dear friend and wise counselor, and we have recently discussed the Stuff of Life, and What Happened to Me This Fall, and why... and whether I'm somehow mentally deficient. I naturally need to know things, and found amazing answers to my questions:

Security. Safety.

Recently while watching the dawn (might explain the afterimage) it occurred to me that there was nothing between me and the sun (read SON) anymore. I do not know why, nor do I know why I didn't always perceive it as so, BUT I now stand entirely responsible for what I do and its effects on the planet. Living life while stripped of all excuses, rationales, complications, etc.- that is an entirely new prospect for me, and it is both terrifying and overwhelming. And I will do it. And the reason is: I have Someone at my back.

Our discussion covered confidence, self-esteem, and courage, and the commonality is that the person developing these traits has a strong parent or supporter to cover him/her. Every trip and fall are covered, a lesson is learned, and character is developed. Now, I don't know why I am only just discovering this, but who stronger a supporter can I have than the Creator of the universe? What better example can I possibly have than God Himself? I have laid out before me the instructions, the path, and the ending. With nothing missing, what else could I possibly do?

I have been blessed with a new and open heart (though sometimes it's amazingly painful- another story, perhaps), and one that is more geared towards people and personalities than before, and I am at a bit of a loss about exactly how to handle it. I have the privilege of learning all things again, like a toddler, and often with the same results as a toddler. But, you know what? What else can I do? I am learning how to live...and generally making a mess as I go along, one way or the other.

I have no fear of ridicule or people mocking me. Here, repeat this and tell me how it sounds: "Look at him- that idiot- paying attention to that person who needs someone to listen to them!" Oh, here's a nice one, also: "Oh, MAN, what a sucker! Giving XXX to that person.

They're taking advantage of you, you dope!" (I know- they sound ridiculous on paper but flow freely through the air.) I have my mission's guidelines already in hand, and know what to do, and as far as generosity: I believe that the problem lies with the person doing the "taking advantage of" and not me, no? I'll let the twisted mind worry about taking advantage of other people after me. Nothing can be taken from me, which I freely give. And what, exactly, do I own, as only a steward of this planet?

How to combat those things, these "dangerous" people? Shall I hole myself up again, and begin again the whole process of dying slowly? Shall I become cold and bitter, and tear down those around me with harsh tone and venomous speech? No, thank you. I have seen- and have done- enough of that already, and have lived that way for far too long.

I will take the ridicule, and the slander, and continue on my wild and sensational adventure, because I know that I am safe, and have an awesome Guide. I am still screwing up, but I'll do it boldly and own it when I do.

And maybe I will have the chance to bless a person or two along the way.

The Walk

I don't care for walking.

There- I said it. Fortunately this note will probably fall into obscurity pretty quickly, with the rest of the post-Christmas Facebook posts pouring in, so it is safe between you, me, and the lamppost.

I walk to a location, with a purpose. There is no "walking to walk, for walking's sake." I was fortunate that my recent foot injury was only temporary, and I can don the Merrell's once again to get down to business, so If I need to move for exercise, I run. Let's face it: I'm a mover and a little hyper at times, so believe me- if I can cover the same steps in half the time, I will, especially since I walk alone. The Fitbit doesn't know any better, and no one notices the 6,000-10,000-step spike, so I feel that I'm safe.

So anyhow, today is the only "off day" in my workout schedule and I can't run, so off to walk (blech) I go with an obstinate pout and a "FINE!" as I leave.

Since I'm new to this neighborhood I decided that my music and I would wander into a local park to scout it out for...when I never go to parks. It's a nice neighborhood and a peaceful park, so it wasn't an unpleasant experience, but I was still only half paying attention because the music was going, and my mind was wandering as per usual- until I reached the clearing.

A gentle rise opened up to a split in the road, and in this split was a clearing. As I reached this clearing, the sun burned through the heavy air, setting it absolutely ablaze as it does after the rain in the summer, tracing lines from the heavens down to the grass. I'm sure my jaw dropped at that point, and I stopped there because I have not seen that bright a sky since I was a boy (and I remember that day), and just stared at it.

Then I knew, and I removed my headset, because it was then that I understood that I was on holy ground. This was no accident, and I was to pay attention. The most apt verse that I can think of for this experience is, "Be still, and know that I am God."

We walked through only a couple of miles of trails, but I understand now.

There's a grand overlook that belongs in a much larger landscape than this park, allowing a beautiful view of the river as it makes its way through our hills, foaming white rapids and all, as it winds through the small valley. I was lucky to be invited to see this when I was, because I think that the leaves will hide the magnificent view in the summer.

The trails reminded me of my first and only trail run, a few years ago. I was sleek and fast on that day, springing from rock to rock, through the brooks and leaves, bounding over trunks and branches at dangerous speed for the terrain. I was sure-footed and alive, with seemingly heightened senses, and ran with the wolves. I will run this trail this year, in my new home, and more dangerously.

And so was I reminded of who I am, who I am not, and what I am to do.

The sounds of traffic returned as I made it out of the woods and onto unknown street a bit farther into the city than I had intended, and I put my headphones back on...but I knew it would be different on the way home.

What I Was Taught

What I was taught

- Distrust of people
- How to study
- How to entertain myself
- How to shape wood (modestly!)

What I was not taught

- How to be a man

- How to fix cars
- How to build a computer
- How to build pretty much anything
- How to hunt
- How to fish

This is going to be an easy one to write, but perhaps a little difficult to narrow down to one or two things on the list, so I'm just going to start verbally vomiting and see where it goes.

I'm the product of a broken home because of divorce, and though I'm not one to blame everything on my parents, I do see some validity in attributing some of my habits to my environment: divorce and a combination of being smart, good in school, and the fat kid for the first seven grades of elementary school. I was regularly made fun of because of one of the latter three, and found that even friends would steal from me (my precious GI Joe gear!) and step-parents would mistreat me. I did learn how to shape wood (but not in the least bit professionally- just to file and chip away at a plank with various tools) from my stepfather, but there isn't much more in my memory than that, and fighting.

What I carry with me to this day- and I am actually grateful for this but don't entirely know the reason for it- is my apparent inability to be a "normal man." I don't hunt or fish, am not a fan of ogling women, and don't know a blasted thing about cars besides where the gas goes and how to shift it (wait- stick shift! That's manly- right?!?). I fondly remember an incident in another state (where hunting is popular and common) where a family friend invited my wife and me to his home, and in the living room of that home he proudly displayed a huge stuffed bear. I of course had to ask about it, and he began to puff up and talk about how he "bagged her at the lake" from maybe 100 yards, with a rifle while sitting in a tree. When I appeared to be unimpressed with his story, he got a little offended, and I explained that I would probably have been more impressed if he took that mother bear down with a butter knife or his own claws rather than a high-powered rifle from a distance.

I don't remember ever being invited back there....

So I have lived my life being a quirky, mostly-unmanly lover of games and books, and though I sport flannel in the winter, I don't have a beard worth discussing. Now that I think of it- someone recently called me "metrosexual" although I do NOT spend a lot of money on clothing or my appearance; I'm a bit too old for that. At any rate: women seem to like me, and men hate me almost on sight, which is an amazing ability that I in no way had to cultivate. I believe that my lack of bravado and the need to swing certain body parts around, in combination with my lack of super-manly stories of beer and sports, are actually threats to them. I see through the lies and egos, question both at will, and pose some weird threat to manhood at large.

It's almost comical in some strange way, as if I see them, and they see me (a la Avatar), and there is an instant disdain, each for the other.

Bring it.

Something Awesome

This is not going to be one of my introspective, melodramatic posts; this time I just want to encourage you- implore you, perhaps, to do something awesome.

My life has recently provided me some opportunities to bless, and be blessed by, a few people in different ways. Many have been the tiniest of events: a cubicle conversation; a cookie (or five) in the office; a new gamer friend. As I'm remembering these events I'm filled with the always-unexpected peace and joy that comes from human interaction- of touching people.

Ok, ok, OK: granted- I can be a ham and attempt to be a charmer (whether or not I succeed is another story, entirely). I openly admit that I tend to favor women, and why not- I have found that in general women like me (or at least tolerate me) and men just plain-old do NOT! I enjoy the social dance, and- let's not turn this into another blog today....

SO: I have had a chance to offer the smallest of blessings to people and have been filled with blessings many times over- and it's not enough. I need more of this "thing", and I will have it. Every now and again I remember the movie Crash, and how one of the actors said that people crash into each other just to experience the human touch. Is it as simple as that? I don't know- perhaps that is some of it. I will tell you that sometimes I am pained by random feelings I get at the Mall, or in public; sometimes nondescript, and sometimes I can almost sense the source of it directly. But no matter.

So my point is: today I grabbed an UNO's gift card, walked up to a table, and gave it to the family seated there saying, "Please take this gift card. I'm a parent, too." Then I just left. I'm tentatively planning the same thing at Starbucks, and the grocery store. I don't have a plan at this point, other than to say that I'm not done with this, and I hope that you're now thinking about doing this as well.

All I can say is Do Something Awesome. Now.

Small Pleasures

I live a life of small pleasures.

I'm not complaining; it's just an observation as I sit at Dunkin' Donuts and look around at the little wonders around me.

I haven't seen every "The Biggest / Smallest / Tallest X" in the country yet, and don't know if I ever will, and that's fine (as an aside: I told myself, in the recent past, that I'd venture to see every extreme that I could: the biggest mall, the other ocean, the highest mountain, the biggest hole- you get the idea). Perhaps much like most people, I work my hours, travel the same route home, take the same route to walk the dog, etc. etc. Again: I'm not complaining- just making an observation.

(Incoming odd tangent alert)

Where does gaming fit into this? Well, I have a bit of an active imagination, and maybe the reason that I haven't done so many of the "real" things that other people do, is that I have traveled far ingame. "Is it live, or is it Memorex?" (if you're old enough to remember THAT ad), and does it matter? In the purely sensory world- I don't know that it matters. My heart has boaten (pulling a little Doug Adams verb conjugation there) a certain number of beats, and I have heard and seen "the world" (virtual worlds) with awe, excitement, or fear, so in that sense- I have actually "been" to these places. I can't even count how many times I've literally jumped out of my chair, with the accompanying yell, when something ingame scares me. So I suppose that, based on my human reactions, these things have "happened." Maybe only another gamer would understand- and even agree- with this.

"But I digress," as the hackneyed phrase goes.

At any rate: if you're a Hashtagger, you'll probably recognize the tags on my social media posts, because I enjoy posting places I've visited because of Ingress, a mobile game that is based on travelling to real world landmarks and locations. Like this Dunkin' Donuts.

The point: the many small pleasures.

The early morning at bagel shop in a neighboring small town, where I got to see a mom having a bagel with her daughter, planning their Easter Weekend Outing.

The downtown college town tour, where I learned just how large and close together those little holes are, that landscapers poke into the ground to aerate the soil. The ground looked for all the world like a million dogs took a million dumpers all over the quadrangle. I've never seen anything quite like it.

The unexpected silent tears over a bagel at another bagel shop, where I (admittedly for the first time) learned that I have terrible trouble with the concept of children in pain (while browsing the World Vision site, seeking a child to support. Maybe this is where my affinity for Extra Life comes into play...).

And now here at Dunkin' Donuts. It's almost embarrassing to say how pleased I was that this DD has outlets with USB chargers at at least six places in the restaurant, and a little fireplace and comfortable chairs. I'm almost warmed to tears writing this as the sun pokes out through the clouds this afternoon and Closer to Fine starts playing on the restaurant's radio. I think it's providence; I hear it and understand.

Time to go and do more little things.

Fur and Phoenix

I glanced down at my latest tattoo and noticed that today is apparently Peeling Day, and realized that this is no normal phase of my healing skin, but it is life grabbing my attention again, telling me a story- spinning for me another tale in ink, steel and skin.

I have, all around me, pieces of those who have voiced the questions that shape me, and by my answers I am molded and made "me." Every action carves away the stone that will in the end be forever my self. I can see the pieces coming together now, its form beginning to emerge into something new and unexpected, and I know that I must take care in shaping it, because I know that it is the last time, and time is of the essence.

The glyph of the phoenix, a new creation birthed from fire, ashes, and death. Its dying screams chill to the bone, piercing the soul and shadowed only by its glorious cry of victory as it rises from the ashes and soars beyond sight.

The mark of the bushi, of honor and glory, duty and discipline.

A bar of steel marks the body and scars flesh, a silent witness to the tales told to the winds, of adventures in faraway places and epic quests of the heart.

The ink of the Horde- a relentless pursuit of victory and a struggle for survival. Feral, merciless, loyal to clan, swift to strike, filling the air with cries of blood, victory, and thunder.

I am scarred. I am pierced. I am pain, and I am healing. My body is being shaped as surely and steadily as my character, into something unforeseen. There is no mystery: something is happening- something surprising and unique, with perhaps a hint of danger. Whatever it is- I'm certain that I won't leave this world as I entered it.

And in this whole story again resurface the wolves of parable, that fight a vicious and bloody battle of claw and fang over the control of my heart and soul. One of pride, guilt, anger, and ego struggles against the one of peace, serenity, compassion, and joy, and as the tale goes: "which one will win?"

"The one you feed."

You see: I am a creature of voice and sound, and ideas made whole in a story and a song. I give voice to visions, and spin tales that wake hearts and stir souls. War is waged, and lives are lost, in my song. Joy and torment dance around these words, a deadly mix for the unprepared, and the hand is mine that knocks the arrow that reigns down both in that song.

The Mall

I'm just sitting here tonight at the Mall doing some homework (hmm- Mallwork?) when I looked up from my work and watched as two people met each other for the first time. I choose to fancy that they first met online somewhere, and chose here, at Starbucks, to meet in person; it's safe, public, and there is plenty around to distract the bored.

Then I sat back and just let the Mall wash over me.

Let me explain.

I've been coming here regularly for about 35 years. I've eaten, drank, met and courted girls and women, and have spent the hours and days watching people come and go here. That alone ties me to this place perhaps a little more than the "average person" who buys their goods and leaves, oblivious to the essence of the Mall.

I see it tonight, and can't help but feel it, because I am in it, and carried by it. This place lives and breathes, and just a tiny bit of each person who visits remains within it: the excited dad who receives his kids from mom for the weekend in their Weekend Kid Swap; the boy who spends weeks' worth of lawn mowing money to invest in the latest game; the man who stands breathless before the waitress with whom he is absolutely smitten, gathering the courage to ask her out for a coffee- just a moment in time that could change lives forever.

I have been here for all of them, and they live in me, and I live in this place. Every body making its way down the walk is the flow of blood that makes this place live. Funny: I looked up again to see a man embrace his woman vigorously, and they smiled at each other and picked up their coffees, and danced their dance of life down the walk. Someone might well be watching me right now, wondering why my eyes fill to tear suddenly, for no apparent reason.

I love it here. My home, my history, my life.

Sad

There's a sadness in me tonight as I sit at the café and look around, and think about this past season. I feel sad for the lonely, and those who are afraid. There are so many souls, silently screaming for peace and comfort; I can see it in what I read, and in their eyes, and almost visibly, in trailing falsehoods and fairy tales of strength and security.

I've spoken to many people in this season's travels- in person, in fonts and screens, and apps and pages. I can see all of them now, and their struggle to be strong, and in control, and independent and brave and modern and carefree in this onslaught of people and posts, of messages and invitations and empty and broken promises.

It's a vast sea of broken people, all struggling in this effort to be themselves, in a world of scavengers and demons. There's a pain that some hide better than others, but all hide in some way or another; it's not safe "out there" and the soul can't truly soar- a person's beauty can't be truly and fully revealed, because there are dark souls among us who would steal that beauty away, and leave behind a spent and empty shell, to bear such pain yet again. Wings are broken and bruised, and bare of the feathers that make them fly, those feathers a path- the wake of a life of trust broken, and love ravaged and lost.

And so we speak words that we don't mean. We fill the air with empty promises, only half aware that someone may truly be listening; it's all about us, after all, and protecting ourselves from anyone, anything, at all costs. We ourselves become that which we're fighting- shallow specters of half-truths and no character.

I can commiserate, because I'm in the same sea, swimming and battling the same evils, ceaselessly, day after day.

But this wolf is not alone.

I'm never alone because with a word I turn a smile, and with the weaving of speech, I have an ally. I've tasted the blood that these souls bleed because in lifetimes past I've caused similar wounds; I know their pain, and I know how to cause it- and how to help mend it. I know that it's not only possible to change this place and boost a heart or two- it's a duty. It's an honor and a privilege to wage this war- to touch every heart that I can, to leave with less of myself because someone else has taken it, and is full. I know I'll err down this path and must hope that forgiveness is not out of reach, but I've done nothing for far, far long enough.

I don't expect anyone to understand, because I don't, myself. But I know it is my time to give of myself until there's nothing left.

I am no longer sad.

A Tale

There once was a man in a faraway land, wandering the fields and towns, always restless, always searching, driven towards some unseen prize without shape or form. Now, one day this man (though only seemingly so, for his appearance belied his antics. But that is a story for another day) happened upon something unexpected by any measure. In a certain small town's marketplace he stumbled upon a princess, the likes of which he had never seen, and he questioned if this woman really stood before him or if he had finally lost his mind, for what a sight! An amazing beauty in a reindeer dress stood before him, a glorious woman in green and red, silken skin and lips appearing tender beyond imagination, the fairest skin imaginable, and hair ablaze to match this wanderer's heart, now set afire with new purpose. How can this be? What sorcery can conjure such a thing beyond beauty?

In the days to come they danced the beautiful dance of the hunter, the wolf, and the queen, sharing stories of old, passions of the heart, and dreams of the future, all over exotic cakes and drink. They would spend their days together, talking, laughing, sharing and learning, and sometimes weeping the tears of sad memories, past trials and suffering that each had born, and carry still. They knew that they each had their burdens, the scars of travel down long and treacherous roads, marks from the past both visible and unseen, but their bond would overcome them all, and they understood that the scars that shape them do not define them.

Days and days again they spent with each other and their families, telling tales over the fire that was always cooking an endless supply of something marvelous to be shared, and to find them playing games until dawn was far from uncommon. There was no shortage of strange and unusual stories and surprises, for the wordsmith had collected both along his long journey to distant lands.

And though their days were filled with laughter and stories, travel and exploring and song, they never tired of each other, and were rarely apart. Be it the bazaar or the plays- our hero was always attentive to his queen, and she, to him. It was not unusual for them to be touching each other in some way, wherever they were- if even a brushing against each other as they walked through the shops. Far from rarely one would see our man stalk his "prey" and embrace his fiery queen from behind, one arm around her waist, and another brushing aside her long hair to expose a neck for gentle- and not so gentle- kisses, as was his wont.

No one knows exactly where our adventurer and his queen have gone, but we know that wherever they are, they will have more stories to tell, and many ears eager to hear them, for who does not love an epic love story? Somewhere you'll surely hear tell of the fireside tales of our hero and the courting of his warrior queen, his shieldmaiden.

Take note of his story, and pay close attention, lad, for to win the heart of a fiery maiden is no easy task; such a woman will not be swayed by brawn and ale. To open the heart of the Valkyrie requires as much character as charm, as this maiden is keen of eye and sees the foul soul of the deceiver for what it is. Be ever aware, ever vigilant, and be sure that you would be lucky to die on the day she has granted you a kiss, because a life without that kiss would be lived in vain.

THREE

BELLA

The mysterious Bella- the destiny, the prize, and the subject of a few of my works. I decided to give her a section of her own.

I can't say when or why I chose "Bella" as the name of my mysterious queen; it may have been around the time of my obsession with the Twilight series. Yes, I saw them- saw them all in one day, as a matter of fact. I rented the first one online one day, watched it, and immediately ran to my local Best Buy to grab the rest of them for a Twilight-athon. There is no shame in that at all, as far as I'm concerned; I'm not sure that I've ever owned any Man Cards, anyways....

At any rate, I'll leave it to you to determine whether it's a person from the past, or the future, or some ideal that I've carried with me along my journey. I fully intend to take the secret to my grave, the truth lost forever, and as dramatic as I tend to be.

The Workout High

The workout high really does exist. It's a great place to be- tired and happy, open and more carefree, if just for a little while. I stand taller and more proud, more manly and strong (at least in my own mind). I can appreciate it. So it made sense that it was then that I would say, "This would be the spot for my queen. She would belong here-in this time, and in this place."

And then I thought about it, and realized that I was wrong.

There's no passion when things are good. There's no cost when people are happy and carefree. There is joy when the spirit dances, but that vanishes with the wind, when the sun passes behind a cloud. What then?

No: I am not for this place, and I was ashamed that I was so selfish and shallow.

I would have my Bella when life is difficult, and we are weary. I would have her where she cries and is lonely, and needs strong shoulders to bear her burden. I would have her pound my chest in frustration, let loose her pain, and lay her down to rest when she is spent, to stand watch again.

That is where the heart is, and where life is lived. That is where the passion truly lies.

The Chair

I love this poem, though I admit that I'm the worst divider of poetry into lines; I just can't decide where to drop the line down, or if and what punctuation is the best for what I'm trying to say. The first draft of this poem was more or less just sentences with more punctuation until I submitted it for that English Comp Class of Death (that I'm sure I mentioned in this book someplace), at which time I split up the words more to make it more like a poem than tiny paragraphs.

This poem always brings to my mind a specific chair, and though I won't put that picture here, maybe you'll conjure the same chair that I do. It's perfect for whiling away the hours in deep conversation.

I hope you enjoy it.

I have a chair that I did not buy and have never touched

but it is my favorite chair.

I don't know how comfortable it is, or the type of wood,

but I can feel the wood warmed by the long, slow summer sun

when we sit catching up on forever.

I don't know where this old chair sits, but I know that it is waiting for us,

and we will find it when it is time.

I don't know when this rest will come

but I have wandered for thirty years

and whatever path is before me is light and easy to travel.

I don't know how I'll find this chair

but I know as surely as the sun favors me

that I will not fail to find it when the time has come.

I have no surer path than that upon which I travel,

for I know the course

and I know its prize.

This is Bella's chair

and she will not be left wanting.

Reawakening

The reawakening of my heart and soul is a mixed blessing, wrenching me in and out of life, and back into a memory randomly, on a whim. I promised myself at the start of this, to venture off with all of my newfound will to live, and to live fully- and I will- but the guide that leads me is cruel and does not yield.

But there can be no failure. Not again.

This relentless host fancies the most random of triggers; on one day a field, on another a spoken word, and today in a song I am jarred out of life, and this time into a gym- a school dance. Only one split second- the draw of the shortest startled breath- leaves me with a brush of hair against my cheek, the curve of the small of a back on my hand, a breath on my neck-

Bella is near.

...and then nothing.

An empty room, a desperate grasp for a memory too fleeting, and a sigh.

Four

THOUGHTS

I separated the following entries into what I consider thoughts rather than just diary or blogging entries; they seemed to have more of a purpose- a speech directed towards someone, if you will.

―——

I Call You Out

This season of life ends, and another begins, and as always I find that judgement awaits me. Is it my own fault for sharing my stories, and therefore calling judgment down upon me? Perhaps; I'm free and open with my beliefs, opinions, and my outlook on life and all of its amazing offerings. I've never considered that a bad thing, but it does pose its problems because there is no shortage of people who will turn their attention from their lives to tear at mine. I'd like to think that I'm not likely to change, either, because I hold the belief that someone may need to hear what I have to say or need to see what I've done- not that I'm so great, or honestly have that much to offer- but perhaps someone needs just the slightest boost of some sort, to help them along their own path.

I often tell stories to elicit some deep and intense feelings, and aggression is typically in the form of regret or some other dark emotion turned inwards. Today, though, things are different. Something has tripped in me, and I don't imagine everyone will want to hear what I have to say.

And that is exactly my purpose.

Life is full of adventures, puzzles, and winding roads, and I intend to take many of them while I can. I guarantee that I will often take the wrong one, and may need to double back just a bit before I continue, but I tell you this:

When I stumble and fall it is because of my own action- no mortal spoon-feeds me the rules and pulls me along. My heart moves the blood that drives me through these woods- *my* heart. There is no acceptable norm that I feel driven to follow and obey; there is no politically correct proverbial nod that I await, led to the end of my life like the rest of the sheep. I fall, and I rise again, with my scars and my stories.

To those who live among the bland and washed-out vanilla masses, waiting for things to happen to them, and essentially just living each day waiting to die- you do not need my permission to do so.

Am I indignant? Perhaps. Rightfully so? I'm not sure, and I don't care. Am I concerned about what people think? Apparently, but not in any fearful uncertain way. I suppose that if there's a point to this rambling today, it's to prop up a mirror of sorts. I stand- sometimes alone, but I stand. Of my own accord, and in no one's shadow.

I call you out today.

May the scent of your soulmate

ever surround you

and your prey be always upwind.

I am known by many names:

Inciter of Shenanigans

Stirrer of Pots

Itch in the Underpants

and it is my time.

Decisions

I have just realized that my roll of aluminum foil has lasted longer than the entirety of my last relationship- from meeting to divorce. So...is this a testament to my wise decision making? Terrible decision making?

Interesting that it appears to be a testament to both my horrible decision making AND wise choices; I shop at wholesale clubs.

Trick Or Treat

Halloween again, and time to paint yourself bloody fang chin trickles, hang skeletons from signposts, and put demon sentries on your doorstep.

No, I'm not going with the flow for this holiday, either (surprise).

I dunno- there's something about the holiday that I am either seeing through, around, or failing to see at all. I am having a hard time taking out my little Satan doll, all cute and impish in his nice little red suit, pointy horns... and isn't that little trident so darling?!? I just can't see it anymore, and maybe it's because I understand that it isn't actually just a toy.

Sure, sure, I can see some amusement in masquerade parties- I think I'd be Spider-Man, myself. Bobbing for apples, socializing, etc. are fun: I get it.

(Fade to Overview)

Christians have what can be a pretty broad and easy principle to follow: either it's from God, or it's not. Just like Anakin Skywalker said, "If you're not with me, then you're my enemy," or something like that: piece of cake. So then, there are things in this world that will either bring us closer to God's will and presence, or send us farther away, and our job is to try to steer away from the bad stuff. That is the not-so-easy part. (I'll be the first to admit: I've watched some movies that I wouldn't want to invite my Savior over to sit and watch with me, even with some nicely-buttered popcorn....)

In that light, what if someone dressed up as their sister, who happened to commit suicide by hanging? Oooooh, that's scary!

What about the drug addict, complete with needles sticking out of both arms? Ow, that's gotta hurt!

Do you have any gamblers in the family? What about dressing up as the kid who didn't have a good meal, or maybe suiting up as the bed with not quite enough covers to keep the child warm, because the gambler spent all of the family's hard-earned money on blackjack? Look, I even painted little shadows under each rib of the costume, for that cool hunger effect!

Ohh, wait, wait: a costume of the goalie that got a skate to the neck and bled out all over the goal crease, back-mounted goal included.

We love violence, wear pretty skulls on our clothing, and turn death and demons into fun playthings and romance movies. Satan isn't something to be feared anymore, and many think he's just an idea. Do this often enough, spread it all around long enough, and pretty soon we're dancing with the devil in the pale moonlight (the movie buffs will get that one).

Maybe it's just me, but I can't look at Halloween without seeing the unglamorous suffering part that the media doesn't glamorize. I can't say that I see anything funny about being kept up by nightmares. I wasn't amused my first night without my boys, during my divorce, when the Enemy was throwing a party for doing his part in breaking apart my family. I didn't particularly shriek like a schoolgirl with the thrill of having to sell my belongings piece by piece when I ran out of money for beer.

Paint me a party pooper.

Remorse

There's a wound that runs deep and spans all time, in the heart of one who has wronged another person.

And it is rightly so.

As the warrior strikes swift and true against those who have wronged him or those in his charge, so should suffering and remorse offer no comfort to him, for those innocents that suffer by his hand.

And this, too, is rightly so.

For the warrior knows right from wrong; it is ingrained in his heart and soul, since only through that can he act as though the course of action he is about to take is the only one that ever existed.

This is the way it should be, I think. I haven't thought enough about how this meshes with biblical thought- if it does at all- but it rings true in a different place. This is a place that requires no pondering; there is no deliberation, no musing or mulling things over- no discussion to be entertained here, because the answer is always clear.

I fancy this as being the heart of the warrior- or the wolf. Whichever it is- it can't be avoided, and it can only be denied for so long before the honorable becomes shamed and without a master.

A ronin.

Battle

God has put battle in the heart of man.

He has filled man's spirit with the unending craving for adventure, and in his soul, the undying desire to fight for a cause, for his woman, and for his God.

I'm not talking about the vile craving for wanton destruction and pain- not that those do not exist- but these things are not of God.

God's sons know there is a Right, a Just, and an Honorable- and will fight for them.

...and should they fall in battle, it would be a good death. There will be tales of it, told by his children, and those left behind who would benefit from it.

Even in failure, that pride and honor of a life well-lived and fought for can never be taken from him.

It's a priceless and eternal gift.

I Am Home

Things are a little busy here again, which is good for me; my mind and attention need to be active and engaged pretty much all of the time, which has proven to not always be great for people around me.

But that's not the point.

It seems that for a fair portion of my life I've typically been apologetic to someone for something: school, relationships, hobbies, etc. The list seemed timeless and endless, and as suddenly as I remembered all of this- it all disappeared.

Just like that.

Today.

So I'm sitting here in my room, with no one to ask, no one to tell, and just...no one.

And it's amazing.

I am on the rise yet again. I have learned from my experiences, and have grown into "me"- I think. But that doesn't matter at this point, because whatever "me" is will continue to be shaped until it is done, if ever. So I sit here this evening unapologetically and say:

I am a Believer.

I am an Extra Lifer and a gamer.

I am the Horde.

I am a Twitch streamer, and terrible at it.

I enjoy the ukulele, and play it as well as I stream.

I have four ocarinas that I play worse than I stream.

I give too much, too frequently.

I am sad for the lonely.

I am honest, and stand strong in my beliefs,

And I am not afraid.

I know my name now. And I am home.

Nothing can be taken from me,

which I freely give.

AFTERWORD

I told you I had a penchant for the dramatic.

About Author

P. Volk was born in the United States in a time that is all-but forgotten: there were no cell phones, joysticks, or Internet for the masses. He grew up in Massachusetts in the era of Pong, the Commodore 64, and The Little Rascals, in a time when life as a child was spent more outside than looking at a screen, which undoubtedly contributed to his creativity and imagination.

Many decades and miles later, Proval returned to and currently resides in Massachusetts, where he still wonders what he will do when he grows up.